The Milky Way Chronicles

C. Baby

Volume 1

The Milky Way Chronicles Volume 1

Copyright © 2024 by C. Baby

ISBN (979-8-9898507-5-4)

Table of Contents

Chronicle 1

Misty Seattle

Pt. 1 The Spark

The Hartsfield/Jackson Airport was a complete madhouse. Sharon hated flying out of here. Her nerves were too fragile for this nonsense. But she loved her job, and they were footing the bill as usual. She arrived at her departure terminal and realized she had some time to kill so she headed to the closest bar to have a drink before boarding her flight. Fox News was on the monitor, and they were discussing the President and his job performance numbers. As she ordered her libation, a strong Long Island Iced Tea, she could overhear someone chuckling seated behind her.

"Ain't that some shit," he stated nonchalantly. "These people wouldn't know a good job performance if it slapped them on the ass." His name was Waliq Gordon III. As she glanced in his direction something caught her eye. There was a cute teddy bear seated in front of him. His phone rang and she returned her attention to the news broadcast. "Here you go ma'am. That'll be $11.50." She paid for the drink and scanned the area for a quiet table. There was an empty booth a few tables behind where Waliq sat. She made her way to the booth and pulled out her laptop to do some final updates to her presentation. Whoa... this drink was really strong but oh so good. Yasssssss!

As she typed away, she caught a snippet of Waliq's conversation... "Yeah bruh, as soon as I land, I'm heading straight for the hotel to check in and change clothes. I need to teach you boys a lesson in fundamentals. Yeah whatever, you suck, ya boy Tim sucks, and ya boss is straight garbage. I'm surprised you didn't get fired the last time I played with y'all." He let out a good laugh and slapped the table. "Alright bruh, I'll hit you up when I touch down. Peace!" He laughed some more and finished his drink. "I'm sorry ma'am, I didn't mean to disturb you." As she looked up, she had to keep herself from choking on her drink.

He stood 5'10, had a warrior's build, smooth mocha complexion, and from where she sat, he was pleasantly endowed. "Oh no, you're fine," she replied. "I meant, no problem." Come on Sharon, keep it together. "That's a cute teddy bear," she said. "Oh yes, thank you," he replied. "It's for my niece. She's turning 4 this weekend." - "Oh ok. I thought maybe it was for your daughter," she said. "Nah, no kids yet," he replied. He looked at his watch; his flight would be leaving soon. "If you'll excuse me, I need to use the restroom. Have a nice flight," he said as he scooped up the bear and darted out the door. She scanned over her presentation one more time, finished her drink, and closed her laptop. She heard her flight's boarding call and made her way to her gate.

"Excuse me sweetie," cried a frail little voice. She was a humble elderly woman with a cane sitting just to her right. "They've called my seat number in 1st class and my knee is really bothering me.

Can you please help me onto the plane," she asked? "Sure", replied Sharon. The attendant scanned their tickets, and they boarded the plane. She helped the lady to her seat. "Thank you, young lady," she said. "You're welcome," replied Sharon. Her seat was in coach, window seat. She settled in for the long flight and grabbed her book.

Waliq knew he shouldn't have ordered those damn enchiladas. They were going to make him miss his flight. Toilets flushed and sinks squealed. He finished up and washed his hands. "Baby girl was nice", he thought to himself. Oh well. He needed to get that load out before getting on the plane. He heard the final boarding call for his flight and made a mad dash for his gate. He was the last one to board. His seat was in first class, so he didn't have far to go.

People were still stowing their luggage and fidgeting about. Thankfully no one sat next to him, so he buckled the teddy bear in and then himself. "That's a beautiful teddy bear you have there," said the lady sitting across from him. "Thank you," he replied. His phone buzzed and he excused himself.

He quickly finished his call and turned his phone off. The plane taxied onto the runway and accelerated quickly. Once airborne, he reclined his seat and dozed off. He worked his ass off for the past month and he needed the rest. Sharon was lost in her book and sipped on another drink. She thought about the guy from the bar. "Wonder where he was going," she thought? The captain came over the P/A. "Good evening passengers, this is your captain speaking." They had no idea they were on the same damn flight.

The 5-hour flight to Seattle was smooth and uneventful. The captain came over the PA once again. "Ladies and gentlemen this is your captain speaking. We are on final approach to Tacoma International Airport. We hope you enjoyed your flight and thank you for flying Delta Airlines." As the plane pulled into the gate, Waliq gathered his things. He noticed the cane sitting next to elderly woman. "Can I help you off ma'am," he asked? "No thank you, young man. There are a lot of people and I'm not as fast as I used to be. I'll just wait for everyone to leave so I can take my time. Besides, my son's arranged transport for me so I'll be fine," she stated.

He departed the plane and made his way for the transportation area. As Sharon approached the door, she saw the lady she helped on the plane. "Hey there", Sharon said to the woman. "Let me help you off the plane," she said. "Are you sure", the woman asked? Sharon was the last passenger to leave the plane besides the old lady, so it was no trouble. As they walked down the gangway the lady casually said, "there was a handsome young man sitting across from me with the most beautiful teddy bear. Some little girl is going to be very happy. Poor man slept the entire flight. He laughed in his sleep, imagine that." Sharon's heart dropped.

Waliq arrived at the luxurious, Four Seasons Hotel. "Good evening, sir, welcome to the Four Seasons. "Will you be checking in with us, asked the clerk behind the counter"? He handed her his ID and credit card. "I'm sorry Mr. Gordon but we don't have a reservation for you in our system," she said. "What," he replied. "That's impossible. I have the confirmation number right here," he protested. She took his tablet and scanned the information on the screen. "OK, give me a few minutes to check something out," she stated. She excused herself and he looked around for a place to get something to drink.

Sharon sat in the back seat of the taxi returning text messages she'd missed during the flight. "Hi mom, I made it safely. Will call you once I get settled in. Headed to hotel," she pecked. "What's there to do here over the weekend," she asked the driver of the taxi? "Awww wow there is lots to do," said the driver with a heavy African accent. "We have the Pike Place Market, the Music Project Museum, oh and of course there is the Space Needle. But there is much more than that. It just depends on what you're in to." They arrived at her destination without incident. 99 Union St.

She stumbled her way to the front. She was in complete awe of the elegance of the hotel. Her job had done well with this pick. As she busied herself with the clerk, the other clerk had returned to her station. "Mr. Gordon, please return to the front desk. Mr. Gordon, please return to the front desk." Sharon signed her receipt and put away her affects. Waliq returned to the front desk, placed the bear atop the counter, and waited. Sharon glanced to her left and became frozen where she stood. Wow! Of all the places. "Hey, how's it going," she asked cheerfully. "Oh wow, hey there," replied Waliq. "You must be Mr. Gordon," she asked? Waliq extended his hand and introduced himself. "Yes, I'm Waliq Gordon III," he declared. "And you are?" "HI, I'm Sharon Gentry," she said with a blush.

They stood in the elevator bay and chatted for a few minutes. As they boarded the elevator he asked, "Would you like to attend a party tomorrow? Waliq had a full day with the family and Sharon had several presentations to give for her company. "So, you must be in the penthouse? I overheard your number," She asked? Waliq chuckled... "Nah but close. My asshole brother cancelled my reservation as a joke, so they gave me an upgrade for the inconvenience," Waliq replied. "Well, this is my floor," Sharon said. You have my number so text me when you're done because I'll probably still be in meetings," she continued. "OK, will do," he replied, and he waved goodbye.

It was 4:52 pm and Sharon was ready to call it a day but unfortunately the current presenter was drag assing his way through his spiel. Her phone buzzed... (Waliq) "Raid the pantry tonight at the Woodmark Hotel. You wanna go?" "What is, Raid the Pantry," she responded? (Waliq) Very nice place plus the food is great and FREE SNACKS!! Google it and let me know," he stated. She did as he asked and Googled the information. Very interesting, she thought. "What the hell," she said to herself. Besides, she had been having thoughts about him throughout the day. Those lips... that beard... his deep voice... Had her kinda moist all day.

"OK sweetie, uncle has to go now but I'll see you tomorrow, ok?" Waliq scooped his niece up in his arms and they gave each other a super tight hug. "I love you uncle Liq," declared his niece. "Thank you for my teddy bear." Waliq grabbed his brother, Maliq, in a headlock and wrestled him to the ground. He grabbed a handful of grass and shoved it into his face. "That's for cancelling my reservation chump," Waliq belted. "OK brother let me up, my bad," replied his brother. They wrestled a bit more before his sister-in-law came outside and sprayed them with the water hose. She and the little girl broke out into historical laughter. "Damn baby chill out. Stop. OK we're done," screamed Maliq.

The brothers just laid there in the yard soaked, wet, and laughing their asses off. They hadn't seen each other in over a year. Waliq was the oldest by 2 years. Maliq was the chief systems analyst for a major tech company, his wife, Charlene, was a charge nurse at Seattle's Children's Hospital. They had one awesomely beautiful little girl, Yasmin Lovie Gordon

"Come on man so we can beat this traffic," Maliq groaned as they pulled themselves off of the ground. "Nah bitch, ride your soggy ass in the back with the cargo," Maliq chuckled. Waliq climbed into the car and began wringing the water out of his shirt onto the passenger side floor. "Fuck you and drive," he replied. They backed out of the driveway, waved goodbye and sped off.

As they made their way onto I-5 North Maliq put on, *Gangsta*, by Young Dro and the brothers relived their days growing up in the SWATS area of Atlanta, GA. They pulled up the hotel and Maliq said in a kind loving tone, "I love you bruh. Now get the Fuck out." The laughed and gave daps. "Love you too bruh," Waliq responded. "Oh yeah, we'll be by around 9:30 to pick you up." Maliq stated. "I might be bringing a guest if that's cool," Waliq asked? "Awe shit. Big bruh done snagged him one," Maliq screamed as he drove off into the sunset.

Pt. 2 The Explosion

7:45 est. Waliq sat on the edge of the bed in his bath towel watching ESPN when his phone began buzzing. "Hello," he said. It was Sharon on the other end. "Hey. I was just about to hop in the shower. You're going? Cool," he returned. "Come on up. I'll leave the door cracked. I'm in room 1012, tenth floor. Exit evaluator to the left. OK, see you then." He hung up and shuffled to the bathroom.

Sharon slid her heels on and checked herself out in the mirror. She wore a beautifully African patterned sundress. Her Quddess perfume smelled like roses and honey in the springtime. Her skin glowed like brown gold harvested from the mines of Central Africa. Her afro was fierce and regal. It shimmered like the crown worn by the queen of Ghana. She was absolutely stunning in every way.

Sharon nervously rode the elevator up to the tenth floor. All sorts of crazy thoughts went thru her head during her brief ride. "What the fuck are you doing? You don't even know this man. He could be some psycho killer on the run or some shit. OK bitch calm down. It ain't that serious. He had a damn teddy bear for God's sake." Ding... she had reached her stop.

Waliq leaned against the wall of the shower and had his own mental moment of Sharon. "Who is this chick? Is this one of Janice's bullshit games? I can't put nothing past that crazy broad," he thought to himself. "Hello. Waliq, it's me, Sharon." He stuck his head out of the shower door and hollered back, "Come on in and get comfortable. I'll be out shortly."

Sharon casually scanned his personal affects he had laid out on the dresser. *Dangote* by Burna Boy played in the background as she made her way to the window. His room had a breathtaking view of the city's skyline. Waliq forgot his toiletry bag and came into the lounge area to retrieve it. Sharon turned around and they immediately got stuck.

Waliq was blown away at her very presence. Her body had the aura of a goddess. Her scent filled the room like an intoxicating gas that rendered him immobile. "Hi," she said. "Hey," he replied. "How do I look? I hope I'm not over or undressed? I've never been to one of these, raid the pantry events," she said shyly. But Waliq was speechless. He stood there looking at her from head to toe. "You are fucking gorgeous," he gasped.

Her feet were beautifully done. Her toes looked like sweet little candies waiting to be sucked. Her skin was supple and smooth as silk. Before he knew it his ole boy started getting primed. She could see it swell beneath his towel. They both blushed. Waliq turned around and quickly went back into the bathroom. Sharon sat down and began to squeeze her legs together. Her pussy was jumping. Her pulse increased. "That man is fine," she gasped to herself. She looked out the window and stared off into space. This was going to be an interesting night.

They awkwardly walked to the elevators and waited for their transport to arrive. After a few seconds of silence, they both broke out into laughter. "Look I'm sorry about earlier. I wasn't expecting you to look so... umm good," Waliq explained. "It's fine," Sharon replied. "And thank you. You look very handsome yourself." Waliq jokingly looked in the hall mirror, rubbed his beard, and said, "well I try. I think I got it right tonight." He gave Sharon a devilish grin and kissed her hand. There was a ding signifying the elevator was approaching. "Your chariot awaits my dear." Waliq gave her a bow and escorted her to the bottom floor.

They had 15 minutes or so before his brother and sister-in-law arrived. They chatted it up while they waited. Sharon was intrigued at his ability to have an intelligent conversation. She also liked the fact that not once did he look at his phone, other than to return a text from his brother. He asked her more questions than any guy she'd ever known. He showed genuine interest in her, what she did, what she liked to read, and her opinion about current events. She was being mentally stimulated like never before.

Maliq arrived and they climbed into the back seat of the Rover. Waliq did the introductions. "Everyone this is Sharon. Sharon, this is my little brother, Maliq and his wife, Charlene." The ladies wore similar styles, so they hit it off immediately. Maliq made eye contact with Waliq in the rear-view mirror and gave him the look that said, "yeah boy, you got you one there."

WizKid's *Sweet One*, came on and Waliq began to sing to Sharon. Little did he know, that was her favorite song. He could actually sing. His deep voice sent chills up and down spine. She felt a strong tingling sensation pulsing through her moist little hideout. He smelled like a blend of cognac and spices. His shirt contoured his muscular physique and his skin smooth like melted chocolate. This man enchanted her, and she couldn't figure out why.

They arrived at the Woodmark Hotel, and everyone exited the Rover. They all sat down and had a delicious seafood meal and talked about everything under the sun. They had a blast raiding the pantry and tasting the various snacks and treats from around the globe. The conversation was getting better and better. He said things to her she'd never heard before. He paid attention to her and treated her the way a woman should be treated. He was polite, funny, and engaging. It would be hard to resist him if he made a pass at her. Shit... she was fooling herself. She wanted to give him the business in the worst way.

As the evening began to whine down and the moon rose higher into the sky, Waliq and his brother indulged in a Champ Millz premium cigar as the crew made their way back to the truck and hit the highway. Sharon rested her back across his chest and got comfortable. Sade swooned over the speakers, "there must've been an angel by my side." Sharon closed her and gripped Waliq's right hand. It was strong and warm. She slowly slid his hand up her thigh and placed it over her hot wet pussy. His finger played with her clit like a master pianist. She got wetter with each note he played. She came so hard that she had to bite her clutch purse to keep from screaming out in pleasure. Yeah. It's about to go down!

Everyone said their goodbyes and the Rover disappeared into the night. "Your room or mine," Waliq asked? "Yours. I like the view," said returned. The elevators were empty. She grabbed a handful of dick and buried her face in his neck. He smelled good. She wanted him badly. Waliq gripped the back of her afro and began sucking on her neck... he slowly tongued his way to her ears and down to her hard nipple. By the time they arrived on the tenth floor she was ready to lose the dress and track of time.

They entered the room and faced each other. Nothing was said... they just stared at each other for a few seconds. Waliq put some slow music on Pandora and walked behind Sharon. He gently kissed the back of her neck and wrapped his strong arms around her and pulled her closer. Tighter. She could feel him growing. His dick throbbed and pulsed on her ass cheek. He slid the straps of her dress over her shoulders and let it drop to the floor. "Damn she was a sexy mutha fucker," he said to himself. "I'm gonna take my time and explore this ass from head to toe," he whispered in her ear.

He continued his finger medley deep within her pleasure paradise. Slow circular infinity loops around her clit made her juices pour out like a bitten chocolate covered cherry. As he caressed her beautiful mocha twins, he gently squeezed her nipple and slid his middle finger in and out of her honey coated hideout.

Sharon reached behind her and with one hand began to undo his pants. She had never been this hot in the ass before. She'd never had a man touch her the way Waliq touched her. The way he lightly kissed the back of her neck sent her into a trance. His fingers found spots deep within her she never knew existed. "What are you doing to me," she asked? His reply was very unexpected. In a deep warrior tone he responded, "I'm 'bout to lock this pussy down!"

That did it. She came hard as fuck. Pussy juice ran all down Waliq's fingers. Her knees almost gave way. Waliq had to hold her up and keep her from falling. She breathed deeply as she made her way to bed. As she sat down Waliq was removing his boxers. "Gat dammit that's a pretty dick," she said to him as he walked closer. It was long, thick, brown, and reminded her of a 3 Musketeers candy bar. So, she grabbed it and proceeded to take a mouth full of dick.

Uhglll.... She gagged.... Uhglll ahhhh... she gagged again. "You good," he asked? "She mouthed a "yes," between sucks. "Good, you forgot a couple a inches," he clapped back. With long slurp Sharon said, "Oh you to talk shit, huh?" "I'm a shit talker," Waliq jokingly sang out. Sharon laughed and continued her duties. This was going to be fun.

Waliq marveled at her skills. Her tongue swirled round and around and around on that spot he liked. She took pride in her work, he could tell. He played in her honey jar as she honored him. He sucked her juices from his fingers. She had a pleasant fruity taste. The scent of peaches laced his nostrils. He pulled back and knelt before her. He took one leg and lifted it to his face. He started at the top of her foot and gracefully kissed his way towards her steaming, jumping, and super wet coota. She lay back on the bed and let him have his way.

What happened next was nothing short of fucking magnificent! He palmed her thighs and spread them open. He got close, very close to it. She could feel his warm breath on her already sensitive pussy. He slowly put his entire mouth on her. Allowing his tongue to lay across the whole honey pot. She went ballistic. He did exactly what he said he was going to do. He took his time and explored her, pleasuring her, catering to her.

His tongue did amazing things down there. 1st the waves came over the clit. Her eyes rolled as she gripped the pillow and bit into it. "Awww shit," she moaned. Next came the plunge. Waliq opened her with his thumbs and dug into her with his tongue. She had never ever been tongue fucked before. She liked this technique. The new he slowly sucked her clit. Her stomach tightened and her toes curled. "Ahhhh yes baby," she gasped. And there it is. She climaxed again and again and again.

Gentle kisses on her belly. A lick here and a nibble there. He was toying with her body, and she loved every second of it. She stared into his eyes and swirled her hips until she could feel him. She was ready for it. Or so she thought. The dick penetrated slowly. Waliq stopped just a couple inches in. Stroke after abbreviated stroke he pleasured her. It was driving her crazy. She wanted the whole thing up in her, but she relished the anticipation. She got so wet. "Awww damn I'm 'bout to come again," she said under heavy breathing.

He grabbed her by the throat and applied a little pressure. He went deeper and deeper and said to her, "I got plenty more dick for you." Hitting spots and tapping walls, he was giving her the business. My Place, by Tweet, wailed in the background. He sucked her nipples and gingerly gave her pussy some much-needed therapy.

Mary Jane, by Ky-Mani Marley, graced the atmosphere. Sharon climbed atop this chocolate warrior and showed her appreciation. This time she took all of him. It was more then she could stand but she took the whole damn dick. She rode him like a Kawasaki doing 120 on I-95. She held on tight and took off.

YCee's, *West Indies*, drifted through the air and the Rasta girl in her put di slow whine pun him. She felt good sliding up and down on his rod. He toyed with her clit and made her pussy throb. She gripped his meaty spear and kangaroo hopped on the dick. Their bodies were in sync. Connected by an unknown but welcome force.

This was one of those once in a lifetime encounters. The energy they shared was nuclear. It was an explosion of two vibes that culminated into a beautifully orchestrated symphony. "Fuck yeah baby give it me," Sharon moaned with pleasure. "I feel it cumming," she continued. Waliq pulled her close and said, "bitch you better not cum yet." That statement drove her fucking bananas. And on Waliq's command they both popped at the same damn time.

She laid across his chest in exhaustion. Both of them breathing heavily, this felt good. It felt like it was meant to be. "OMG what in the hell just happened," Sharon said while laughing. Waliq got up and retrieved a little treat his brother had given him at the Woodmark Hotel. "You smoke," he asked while dangling a sack of the good green? After they smoked a couple of spliffs and talked for another hour or so, they drifted off into a deep coma like sleep.

Waliq awoke the next morning to an empty bed. He sat up thinking to himself, "damn this bitch done robbed me." Wallet, cash, laptop, everything was still in its place. He looked for his phone and then remembered he'd left it in the bathroom. As he walked through the door a huge smile appeared on his face. On the mirror was a message written in lipstick and a note lying on the counter. THE OLD LADY WAS RIGHT. YOU DO LAUGH IN YOUR SLEEP!! LOL. The note simply read, "You better call me when get back to Atlanta, sir. I really enjoyed you and look forward to seeing you again! Kisses.

To be continued…

Chronicle 2

Catfish & Orgasms

**The brain has a funny way of processing stimulation. There is no written standard as to what one is attracted to or what turns them off or on emotionally or sexually. This tale gets a little messy, but… This time, messy is a powerful seducer. **

Thursday

Theo Banks was an easygoing, laid-back brother. His divorce had just been finalized and his friend, Darnell, wanted to throw him a, "it ain't nothing to cut that bitch off", party to celebrate. Darnell was a clown of the highest order but loved his homeboy and hated his ex-wife. Theo reluctantly agreed to have the shindig at his house since she had taken all of the furniture anyways. "Bruh, you free now. The wicked witch has retreated back to her hellish lair and never to be heard from again, hopefully." Darnell had no filter, but he meant well. Darnell was present during a number of arguments, which lead him to label her, the grand agitator.

Theo arrived at his job where he worked as a sound engineer for a local news station. He loved his job and got along with most of the people there. He'd worked there for about 3 years now. That's longer than his marriage lasted. There were 4 people in his department, and they were a tight knit crew that hung out after work some days. "Morning everybody. I have some great news. My divorce is final," he announced. He continued. "This weekend I'm throwing a little celebration at my house, and you all are invited." The 4 coworkers all clapped and cheered and committed themselves to attending.

At lunchtime he sat at the mixing board, snacking on a bag of chips. Gail, the production assistant, walked in and sat down. "Theo, do I need to bring anything to this little party of yours," she asked? "To be honest with you I have no idea what you should bring. My friend Darnell is planning this thing, not me," he replied. "I'm just hosting it. I have no furniture, but I also don't have any more headaches, so, go figure.

Gail laughed and shook her head. She'd known Theo the entire 3 years he's worked there. Hell, she's known him longer than his ex-wife. They had always been cool but never any funny business. She thought he was a great person to know and deserved better than what he had dealt with for the past 2 years of his marriage. She'd witnessed his ex-girlfriend flip out on him in the parking garage because he worked overtime during major newsbreaks. "Well, sorry things didn't work out," Gail said as she exited the control room.

On the way home from work he got a call from his dad. "Hey son, what do you have planned for Saturday morning," he asked. "Nothing so far, dad. I'm having little get together with some friends in the evening, but the day is free," replied Theo. "OK good. Let's take the boat out on the lake and snag a few out of the water. Help get your mind off of everything," his dad suggested. "Sounds like plan to me. I'll be by the house say around 7 in the morning. Kiss mom for me. See ya." Theo hung up, turned his car off and retreated indoors.

Friday

"Good morning gang. How's it going," Theo asked as he sat his rucksack down and removed his hat? Two of his coworkers had to cancel due to previous family obligations. The other two, Gail and Seymour, were still on board. "Ok, Gail you bring the drinks and Seymour you bring the wings and salad. Darnell is taking care of everything else. I'm going fishing Saturday morning so hopefully we'll get lucky."

"So, what are your plans," asked Gail? "No clue. We've been separated for almost 6 months.

I've just been taking it one day at a time," declared Theo. "Well, I've got a single friend you might be interested in," Gail stated. "Fuck no. That's how I ended up in this mess. A hook up from a relative. No thank you. I prefer to do my own hunting," Theo boasted. "Well excuse me Mr. Wilderness man." Gail had a good laugh off of that one. "OK, I'll leave my friend at home," Gail said as she giggled.

Theo made a few calls and gathered his things to go home for the weekend. He wasn't sure if this party was a good idea or not? He was glad to be free but wasn't quite ready to be on the market again. He was in school part-time working on his Master's degree and didn't want any unnecessary distractions. And he's learned that the wrong woman can be a major distraction.

Saturday

Buzz buzz buzz buzz.... Theo slapped his alarm clock and silenced the screaming little gadget. Dammit man. Theo buried his face into his pillow for a few more seconds before he rolled out of bed at 5 a.m. He washed up, ate breakfast, and gathered his fishing gear. For a second, he thought that his ex-wife had taken his fishing rods. Hell, she took everything else. Then he remembered they were in his dad's garage. He hopped in the car and sped off.

His dad was waiting outside securing the boat to his truck. Theo parked his car in the driveway and went into the house. "Hey ma, what you doing," he belted loudly. His mom was in her study looking over some papers. "Hey son. Come give me a hug," she said cheerfully. "How are you holding up," she asked? "I'm good. Everything has been finalized and I'm a free man again," Theo happily declared. She stood up and gave him a tight hug and said, "Son, I love you more than you'll ever know. You deserve much better and better is out there."

She reached into her purse and pulled out some money and handed it to him. "$20? Really ma? I make $85k a year. I'm good," Theo stated while laughing. "I know baby. Well, take your father to lunch or something," she replied. Theo said, "I love you" and headed outside. "Come on son. I want to beat this traffic. They hopped into the Chevy pickup and drove off. Theo needed a little R & R, it was just what the doctor ordered. He always loved going fishing with his dad as a boy and nothing has changed. He could always count on his dad for some straight to the point advice and a dose of realism.

"Dad," Theo began. "I wonder if I did everything I could, you know, to make it work?" Even though Theo was happy to be free of the endless bullshit, he really wanted his marriage to work. Theo had never been the play the field type of brother. He always admired his folks for the marriage they had. His dad sighed, took a pull of his Champ Millz cigar, adjusted the rearview mirror, and began speaking like a father does.

"Son, women are very strange creations to understand. Your mother and I had our issues. We had our days of not speaking to each other. We argued and cussed. But we had an understanding. Neither one of us wanted to go back and live with our parents so we had to make it work." They broke out into laughter and that made him feel a lot better. "But son, I think you did everything you could under the circumstances. You can't please everyone and like your grandfather used to say, "Don't make no sense chasing something you can't catch."

They arrived at the lake and got the boat into the water. They chatted some more about how the NFL was treating Kaepernick. His dad spoke frankly and said, "America doesn't like the truth, son. She gets very uncomfortable with the truth. Anybody who upholds injustice and senseless death is pure evil. They lack the one thing that makes them human, a soul. Now that man is raked thru the coals because he's tired of seeing innocent young black men die at the hands of an institution that kills without remorse or accountability. Now ask yourself. What the hell did he do wrong? Absolutely nothing. This country was founded on evil, and its so-called patriots are the minions."

The fish were biting and so was his dad. His dad served in the Air Force during a time when it was really hard for blacks in this country. When he returned from Korea, he stopped at a general store in Tennessee while he was in uniform, and they told him he was not allowed to shop there. His father told the clerk that he had fought for this country. The clerk simply replied, "Well you're back in America now boy so get with the program." His dad slapped the guy so hard it knocked a wad of tobacco out of his mouth and told the clerk, "That program doesn't work," and walked out.

Before they knew it, they had snagged close to 30 fish... a few bass but mostly catfish. They headed for the docks and prepared to end their monthly father and son fishing excursion. "Hey, I'll keep the catfish. I'm having a little get together at my house later and this will be perfect," Theo said. They arrived back at his parent's house, and they said their goodbyes. He was ready for a shot of something strong and a nap.

That Night

Theo was helping Darnell with the boxes of liquor and food. It was 7:45 pm and people would soon begin to arrive. "Exactly how many people are coming to this thing bruh," Theo asked? "Darnell jokingly replied, "other than the strippers, about 10 people," Theo's phone went off, "What up," he answered? It was Gail. "So, did you catch anything," she asked? Awe man that's my favorite. Ok I'll stop and get the juices and snacks and I'll be right on. Bye."

"Bruh, check this out," Theo called to Darnell. "We caught so many fish it's like Jesus was in the boat with us." Theo prepped his area next to the kitchen sink so he could clean the fish. He carefully laid out all of his carving and filleting knives. He put on an old college tank top and an apron, which read, "I Fucks It Up in the Kitchen." Theo had learned to cook from his mom and excelled in culinary classes in high school. It was safe to say that he could indeed, fucks it up in the kitchen.

Guests gradually poured in, and the place began to liven up. Theo was positioned behind the breakfast bar cleaning fish. Gail and Seymour arrived at the same time and came in very loud and unruly. Theo loved it. Gail went into the kitchen and placed the party items on the counter. "Get a stool and have a seat," he said to Gail and Seymour. "Can I help with anything," Gail asked. "Yeah sure. Grab the seasoning and flour out of that cabinet and the bowls are under there," Theo replied.

Seymour looked at Theo with a puzzling look and said, "Bruh, what the hell are you going to do with that hatchet?" Theo snapped back, "That's for the heads." "What heads," Seymour asked curiously? "Catfish have thick bones, so I use the hatchet to chop the heads off. Let me show you, "Theo explained. Gail was pouring the flour into a bowl when the 1st chop came down.

She had never actually seen anyone prepare fish from catch to plate. It was something about the way he executed the task of beheading the fish. One by one as Theo retrieved a fresh fish from the cooler, he meticulously severed each with calculated precision. She noticed something else as well. For the first time ever, she saw Theo in a very different light. She knew he was smart, witty, and a guru at the production booth. But she had never seen the hunter in him before.

Theo went about the task of severing heads and gutting the fish like a Samurai Warrior. He was skilled with a knife. He paid no attention to the splatters of blood on his face, neck, and chest. Oh, his chest... It was ripped. His broad sculpted shoulders flexed with every decisive blow. This shit was turning her on. She sat and watched in amazement as this man sliced thru an army of water creatures. She felt her sugar shack begin to throb with every direct impact. Her toes got all tingly observing this hunter at work.

Theo finished processing the day's catch and cut the fish into nuggets. He battered them and dropped them into the deep fryer. Gail liked to see a man that knew his way around the kitchen. Now she knew why his apron bore the inscription it did. She wondered what else he was able to... fuck up?

Gail was on her 3rd wine cooler when the food was ready. She bit into the fish and was pleasantly surprised. It was very good. This was even more of a turn on to her. This man got all bloody and soiled in order to prepare this fantastic tasting meal. "What kind of woman wouldn't appreciate a man like this? His ex is obviously a very selfish and stupid woman," she thought to herself.

As the evening started winding down and guests began to head to the clubs or back home or wherever, Gail realized she was horny as fuck. She had been single for about 8 months now and buried herself in her work to keep her mind busy. Her ex-boyfriend was a complete loser. She hates the fact that she wasted 3 years of her life waiting for a promise that was never delivered. Tonight, made her realize that she was ready to move on with her life. Tonight, she was going to give Theo the business.

"I'll help you get this place cleaned up," she said to him. Theo closed the apartment up and turned-on YT Music. Tweet radio station played a slew of classic slow jams that had both of them signing and working. Gail watched him move about tidying things meticulously. She couldn't help but bite her lip as he danced and swayed to the rhythm. "I'm gonna hop in the shower and get this stink off," Theo said as he disappeared into his bedroom. Gail leaned against the counter and pondered her next move.

She walked to his bedroom and stopped herself short of grabbing the doorknob. She debated with herself as to what to do next. The professional coworker side of her wanted to grab her things and make a beeline for the car. The horny, coota dripping, blood lusting freak in her wanted to go in there and turn all the way up. The freak side won!

Gail slipped into his bedroom and removed her clothes. She stood there as Jill Scott's, *Until Then*, began to play. Was this a sign? Yasssss bitch!!

She could see him through the crack in the door. His dark skin glowed in the soft light. His back was strong, and his legs were like bundles of steel rods. He turned to the side, and she got great view of his profile. He was long and thick. She reached down and touched herself. She was wetter than a rainy summer in central Florida. Watching him made her pussy jump uncontrollably. She relished it. She couldn't turn away. "Ahhhh," she whispered as she made herself release 8 months of anger and loneliness.

Time N Attention, from Rema & Chris Brown hit the air. Gail slipped into the bathroom just as Theo turned the water off. She anxiously awaited him to exit the shower. She was about to explode. That pussy was so hot it contributed to the room full of steam. When Theo stepped out and he was startled to see Gail standing there... naked. He looked at her from head to toe and was in utter shock. Gail was sexy as fuck. He instantly got hard. Gail looked down and her eyes widened as he grew bigger and bigger. Before she knew it, she had cum again.

Theo stepped closer to her, gripped her waist, and pressed his hot wet body against hers. She almost melted. She could feel him, his hardness, and his pulse. He gently kissed her neck. Her sugar shack got juicy she could feel it running down her thighs. He kissed her passionately and he took the head of his dick and played with her clit. He slid his entire rod back and forth across her soft, warm, creamy honey pot. She wrapped her arms around his neck and lost herself in the moment of pure ecstasy.

Theo sat down in a chair his ex-had purchased but failed to take with her. Oh well. It was about to be put to good use tonight. Gail stood there for a few seconds. The steam danced around her beautiful thick body like a celebrating tribe. Those curves. That enchanting Nubian flavor that coated this heavenly vessel... The Most

High truly did a fine work. She walked towards him slowly. Theo patiently took it all in. He was harder than the chances of a black man trying to get a business loan from his local bank. Yeah, he was that hard.

Gail knelt before him as if she were pledging her allegiance to her new king. She looked him in his eyes as she grabbed his royal staff and began to gently kiss it. She started at bottom of his shaft and worked her way up. She desired Theo more than she initially thought. When she got to the top, she concentrated on that spot just below the head. She began to suck it with the attention a bomb finder gives a live IED attempting to defuse it. Only this time she wanted the explosion. She put that damn infinity move on him. Before you know it, sploosh! Theo detonated and Gail put the whole dick in her mouth. It drove his ass bananas.

She straddled him and slid him in... all of him. She felt every inch. Her honey pot gave him a delightful massage. Gail twirled her hips and got acquainted with Theo's big dipper. Theo embraced her within his strong arms and took her milky paps of flesh into his mouth. His tongue played with her nipples like a fat kid with a lollipop. He was deep inside of her. He gripped her pretty round brown ass and began to give her the type of loving only a true Mandingo warrior could give to his warrior queen. He could feel every muscle as her walls gripped him. As they both were about to cum, she pressed her face softly against his and whispered into his ear, "I'll take care of you from now on baby."

Chronicle 3

Birthday Boy: Celebration Fit for a King

It was one of your typical rainy ATL days. Traffic was a mess, and every freeway was gridlocked. Cory was about to clock out in about an hour or so and he could hear customers complaining about the weather and the slowness of the journey getting to the shop. Cory really didn't give a shit because today was his birthday. Well, to be honest he really didn't give a shit any day but today was different. He was 35 today and all he could think about was the lobster and steak dinner his girlfriend was preparing for him.

"Hey Bae. I'm just leaving the grocery store and I'm headed to the liquor store to get your favorite. See you when you get home. Love you," the message read on his cell. Cory was a computer repair tech and loved his job, the customers, not so much. He got a few calls from his family and friends wishing him happy birthday. A customer came complaining about her keyboard not working. Upon further inspection he found the culprit. "Ma'am, there's syrup in your keyboard. You need to buy a new one," he explained. "Well, can't you fix it? Ain't that what y'all do up in here," she blasted back?

Cory just smiled and kindly stated, "We have a few nice keyboards you can purchase over there on the shelf. Let me know if I can help you choose one." She rolled her eyes and walked over to the shelf. Cory looked down at his watch, "30 more minutes, fuck," he said with agitation.

Karlene had been waiting anxiously for Cory to leave for work that morning. She had been making preparations for his 35th birthday for over a month now. Cory worked hard and was excellent with her kids. He stepped in and filled a void and has never complained one day since they started dating over a year ago. Her son loved him. He even started referring to him as his dad. Well daddy was about to get a very special gift this year.

The weather was awful. People drove like pure idiots whenever it rained. This was ridiculous. Cory called up one of his homeboys that lived just off the next exit. He decided to go chill out until traffic died down. He pulled up at Randy's apartment and blew the horn. Randy stuck his head of the door and yelled, "Come in nigga, damn."

Karlene had been tracking the delivery of his surprise gift for the past 3 days. Around lunchtime that day she got a text stating that his gift had arrived. Before she went to the grocery store, she retrieved the gift and took it home and got it prepped for his arrival. She was more excited about his birthday gift than he would be, she thought. He had no idea he was getting it and she did a great job keeping it a secret.

Randy had just finished rolling a blunt and was about to roll another. "Let me roll that one and you keep that one," Cory said. Randy looked puzzled for a second and then said loudly, OH SHIT. THAT'S RIGHT. IT'S MY DAWG BIRTHDAY!" They broke out laughing and Randy grabbed the remote and cranked up the tunes. *Get Loose* by, T.I. thumped through the small 1-bedroom apartment. "We need to hit the strip club and get some drinks with the crew tomorrow night," Randy said excitedly. "You already know pimp," replied Cory. They proceeded to get their smoke on, sat on his patio, and talked shit for the next couple of hours.

Karlene received a text from Cory stating he was at Randy's house until traffic died down. That was perfect because she was a little behind schedule. She got wrapped in a conversation with a friend discussing his surprise gift. She was ecstatic. She couldn't wait for him to come home and see it. She sampled a little bit after she laid it out for display. Mmmm... very tasty. She threw the lobsters on to boil and tidied up a bit before taking her son to her mom's house.

Once back home, Karlene called Cory to see where he was. "Hey baby. I'm about to leave Randy's house in a few. I gotta stop by the auto parts store and get a tag light then I'll be headed home," Cory said. They hung up and Karlene put the steaks on. The potatoes were almost done baking and all she needed to do was shower and get dressed. "This is going to be the most lit birthday he ever experienced," she said to her friend.

Cory walked in and dropped his keys on the table by the door. "Karly," he called out. Karlene came out of the bedroom, shut the door behind her, and lovingly greeted her man. "Hey baby. "I miss you so much," she said as she kissed him all over his face. "How was your day," she asked? "Other than the aggravating ass customers, no issues," he retorted. Cory headed for the bedroom and Karlene quickly stepped in front of him. "Baby I need to wash my hands. The food smells good and I'm hungry as a muthafucka," Cory exclaimed. "Wash your hands in the kitchen baby, I need to straighten our bathroom up," she replied.

Karlene began to make his plate while he washed up. Cory sat down and kicked his shoes off. Karlene placed his plate and drink down in front of him, kissed him on the forehead, and grabbed his shoes. He started to make light work of the lobster 1st and Karlene disappeared into the back. Cory took a swig of his favorite drink, Hennessey and cranberry juice. This is what he needed at the end of a day like today. A hot meal and a lil something to sip on.

They both sat down and had a nice enjoyable dinner. She gave him his first round of gifts as they ate. He received a new watch, a bracelet, and a $25 gift certificate to The Varsity, which was by far the best gift in his opinion. They drank some more and laughed at one another's silly antics and corny jokes. Karlene finished dinner up with a homemade lemon pound cake. After Cory devoured a couple of slices, Karlene rubbed shoulders and softly said, "Now let's go get you prepared for your big surprise." Cory looked puzzled and replied, "What big surprise?"

She led him by the hand to the bedroom. The door was closed. Karlene turned to him and whispered," Baby, just know that I love and appreciate everything you do for us. I got you this last gift because I want to share a part of me you never knew." They hugged and kissed passionately. Karlene stepped to the side and gestured for Cory to enter the room. Cory opened the door and immediately dropped his jaw. He wasn't ready... Lawd knows he wasn't ready.

Now if you had told Cory he was going to be having this type of 35th birthday he wouldn't have believed *it in a million years. Imagine a kid being told they could eat all the ice cream they wanted from their favorite shop. Yeah, that's the look Cory had splattered on his face when he walked into the room. Ok, let's continue.* *

The room Cory left this morning was not the room he returned to. It had been completely redecorated. Karlene had painstakingly created the atmosphere of a king's bedchamber, reminiscent of the mighty, King Mansa Musa. The walls were draped with silk fabrics. The room was filled with the aroma of spices found in the ports of Egypt. Candles lit the room with a dim lustful haze. The king size bed was laced with gold satin sheets and adorned with black rose petals. Gwarn featuring Burna Boy reverberated through the room. Setting the atmosphere for a wonderful night. But that wasn't all.

Karlene raised her hand and snapped her fingers once. Out of the bathroom walked an absolutely breathtaking sight. The gorgeous black angel stood 5'8 tall. Her naturally curly locs fanned out giving her silhouette a goddess pose that could stop a hundred strong men in their tracks. She wore beaded bracelets and neckpieces. Nothing else. Her poppy garden had been cleanly manicured as well. Just like he liked it.

"This is Vivian. She's here to serve you this evening," Karlene proclaimed. And with that Vivian took Cory by the hand and led him into the bathroom where an equally impressive scene awaited him. She began to slowly undress him, starting with his work shirt and then his tank top. "Now put some icing on those muffins," Karlene ordered. Vivian gladly obeyed and ever so gently began to kiss his stone like chest. Lightly rubbing her fingers up and down his chiseled torso.

A hot bath was prepared in his honor. Vivian finished undressing Cory and he stepped into the bathtub. Vivian followed. She sat on the edge and reached for the washcloth. Karlene lit a blunt and handed it to Cory. He leaned back and inhaled deeply. Vivian washed his head and face. Next, she bathed his neck and shoulders. She squeezed warm water onto his chest and lathered him soap. Karlene sat at the end of the tub and observed. She was wet and oozing with excitement and was ready to fuck both of them.

*Let's rewind for a second, back to the good old days with Vivian. Before her failed marriage and her subsequent introduction to Cory. Karlene and Vivian were roommates back at Spelman College. Vivian was a spicy eclectic free spirit from Chicago. She was in the Air Force and had been reassigned overseas for quite some time. She and Karlene had more than a few flings in their younger days. Only time and opportunity separated them over the years. She was more than willing to come thru for a good friend in need. *

Karlene ordered Vivian into the tub to give Cory a foot massage. Vivian complied while Karlene massaged his shoulders. Cory continued to smoke his blunt and sip his drink. Both women broke into simultaneous signing with the next song, *HRS & HRS* by Muni Long. Cory sat back took it all in. He truly felt like a king this night. Karlene did herself. He was in the presence of two very beautiful women, and they were both his for the evening. He was about to give both of their asses the unfiltered business.

The bath and massage were exactly what the doctor ordered. He stood there as Vivian dried him off. Karlene had a bottle of oil warming on the dresser. Vivian ushered Cory to the foot of the bed where both ladies applied oil to his body. Karlene anointed his head with a few drops and graciously rubbed his face and shoulders. Vivian covered his back and legs. Cory began to rise to the occasion.

Karlene continued to orchestrate the evening. She sat and pulled him down onto the bed. She took his pretty penis in her hands and motioned to Vivian to come and sample him. Vivian cupped his nuts and started kissing the head. Cory's soldiers jumped with every peck. Her tongue was warm. It felt good sliding up and down his bridge. Vivian's pussy was dripping in his palm as he toyed with her. She got excited. She sucked him with anticipation. "Slow down. He likes it slow," Karlene commanded.

Up and down, up and down. Damn she was good. She was really good. He kissed Karlene as he toyed with her passion platter. He was in a zone. This was a once in a lifetime affair and he wasn't about to fuck it up. Both women moaned with pleasure. Karlene took her turn. She gave him slow sensual attention. He grabbed Vivian by the legs and sat her on his face. He took a mouth full of pussy. Vivian was soaked. She creamed all over his beard as his tongue joyfully danced deep within her. Karlene smacked her on the ass and sent shock waves all thru her body. Vivian came instantly. She gripped her plush titties and squeezed her nipples. The level of intimacy was cosmic.

Cory laid both ladies beside each other on their backs. He was about to work them out and OVER! He lay on his side and slid into Vivian. He pulled Karlene closer and wrapped her long thick legs around his head. His head rested on her creamy thigh and took his time and ate that pussy like warm piece of apple pie. He was deep inside of Vivian. She locked her legs around his and drove him deeper. Both women came again and again.

After Karlene got off a few times she left to go retrieve some cold water from the fridge. Before she left, she ordered Vivian to mount Cory. "Ride him slow until he nuts and take all of it," she declared. Vivian hopped on the dick with exuberance. Ooh damn she could feel him touching her spots. With every stroke she gushed more and more. She was dripping all over his nuts.

He pulled her close and took her plump nipples into his mouth. He gripped her ass and began to grind on her walls. D'Angelo swooned in the background with *Really Love*. His motions were coordinated with the thumping jazz bass. The vibrations of bass added a higher level of sensation within her. She screamed out with passion, and he let out a gladiator's growl and they both came... at the same damn time.

Karlene was standing just outside peeping in thru the crack. She was pleased at her friend's performance and abilities. She walked in and placed the tray on the dresser. Vivian lay atop Cory and breathed heavily. "Take her there, baby," she said to Cory. He smacked Vivian on the ass and with both hands he locked around her waist. He went about the task of fucking Vivian into another dimension.

Vivian began to see stars as she started to cum again. "Fuck me daddy yes," she moaned.

Cory slid deeper and took longer strokes. Vivian lost it. She couldn't stop shaking. Her honey bubble burst all over Cory. She rolled off of him and collapsed at the foot of the bed. Karlene gave Cory a high 5 and said, "damn baby I just had to sit back and watch you do what you do." She gave him a big kiss and handed him a glass of ice water.

Cory and Karlene sat in the bed and shared a blunt. They talked about some miscellaneous things about their day and made plans for the next. Vivian started snoring and the two of them looked at each other and broke out into hysterical laughter. Karlene shook Vivian's head and jokingly commanded, "Bitch take your ass in the living room with that shit." Vivian staggered to the door and exited. Cory and Karlene finished their blunt, cuddled close, and completed the freak fest, without Vivian. "Happy birthday baby."

Chronicle 4

Shawty from the Dek

The moon hung over Decatur, GA, like a giant having its light dimmed by the passing clouds. It was a cool October Friday night and ATLiens cruised the streets in their candy-coated spaceships playing the latest jams from the crappiest artists. Anyways... DJ Chap had Club Galore LIT. The dance floor seemed to shake with every 808 signature and the crowd responded with elaborate body jerks and booty drops. Celeste Braithwaite was one those perspiring souls.

Celeste was a 26-year-old sister who made the most of her weekends. She moved to Atlanta from a small town outside of Little Rock AR. She was a recent graduate of Emory University Law School and dedicated her weekends to blowing off steam from her job with DeKalb County. Every outing was accompanied by her 2 besties, Tiffany and ShonDrika. These 2 ladies were, shall we say, a little thotty. Celeste on the other hand was a closet thot. We'll get to that a little later.

The ladies danced in their ritualistic circle while chanting the lyrics to their favorite tunes. "Girl, I'm hot. I'm going to get a drink and sit for a few," Celeste screamed into their little huddle. The ladies departed the dance floor in a single file line. At the bar, each sister ordered their drink and rested their feet. Tiffany leaned over to Celeste and whispered, "Check out the rude boy at the end of the bar." Celeste looked and replied, "Yes girl he's been here off and on for the past couple of months. I think it's the owner's cousin or something. But yeah, he can get it."

The dread-headed rude boy they are referring to, Ishmael Hardwick. The brother stood 6'2, cinnamon skin, and locs that smelled like coconuts and paradise. Celeste was correct; he was the owner's cousin. Ishmael hailed from Baltimore

MD. He had recently relocated to the area to assist his cousin with the promotions for the club. He was good at what he did and managed to increase the overall popularity of the club greatly in the past few weeks. He was definitely an asset to the organization.

As Ishmael made his way behind the bar, Tiffany called the bartender to come over. The bartender was a beautiful dark skin woman with a savage afro. "Hey Candace, what's the deal with the brother with the locs," Tiffany asked? "That's my cousin, Ishmael. He handles the promotions for my brother's club. Why, you want an introduction," she shot back? "Girl no, I have a man. I'm asking for Celeste since she's still single," Tiffany said while teasing Celeste. Celeste almost spit her drink out in shock and fired back, "What in the hell are you doing chic? I don't need your matchmaking services, thank you."

Ishmael approached the group of women and spoke. "Good evening, ladies. I hope you're enjoying yourself?" The 3 ladies returned the salutation and commenced to quench their thirsts. Ishmael left the bar and headed for the DJ booth. The ladies returned to the dance floor to finish the night with a few more dances before going to Waffle House like they always do. A crowd of guys was celebrating someone recently being released from prison. Needless to say, they were a tad bit turnt up.

Celeste felt a tap on her shoulder. She turned around and was face to face with a brother that obviously had a few too many shots of gin. "Damn baby you gotta be the baddest in here," he slurred. Celeste said, "thank you," and turned around. That must've agitated buddy because he grabbed her arm and spun her around. "Bitch don't turn yo back on me," he mumbled in her ear. She jerked away and screamed, "Don't touch me you creep." The guy grabbed her shirt and slung her backwards. Before her friends could intervene, Ishmael was knee deep in buddy's ass.

A major commotion ensued, and the girls were whisked away by a member of security. All Celeste heard was Ishmael yelling at the guy. "Fuck boy you don't hit women." She could see blows being swung and bodies being tossed. The police that were posted just outside of the club rushed in and called for backup. The ladies stood across the street by their cars and observed. "Girl what is wrong with people OMG," Tiffany asked?

After several minutes police began to clear the building and started escorting people out in handcuffs. The ladies were shocked to see Ishmael in cuffs. Celeste immediately ran over towards them but was intercepted by an officer she knew. He pulled her to the side. "Listen I know you may know some of these guys but let us do our investigation," he stated. "Look. I was right there, one of the guys didn't do anything wrong," she replied. "That may be, but we still need to take everyone in to get statements. Besides, you can do more for them from the other side," the officer fired back. With that he walked off.

Celeste went home and sat on her couch for few minutes to gather her thoughts. Her hands were still shaking from the adrenaline rush earlier. She'd never been that close to a fight before. She pulled off her Remy wig and peeled off her eyelashes. She replayed the event in her head over and over. She particularly thought about Ishmael. That brother came on the scene like a West African gladiator. It brought a smile to her face, and she felt a tingle in her peach. Something about a brother defending you without being asked to. She had to help him however she could, and she was in a position to do just that.

As Celeste lay in her bed, she twirled her curly locs around her finger and stared at the ceiling. She could not get her mind off of Ishmael.

She wondered what it would feel like to be wrapped in those strong arms of his. The way he dealt with that dumbass sparked a little fire inside of her. The only man to ever stick up for her like that was her father. She pulled out her laptop and logged onto Facebook to see if he had a profile. There it was, she found him.

She scrolled through his timeline and flipped thru his pics. "Awww how cute," she said when she came across a photo of him and his daughter. She looked to be about 3 or 4 years old. There was no sign or mention of a girlfriend or wife. Well, well, it seems that Mr. Ishmael is an educated felon. From what she could piece together he did some time for minor drug possession. That little incident happened before he got his degree. At least he's taking advantage of his second chance and changing his life for the better. Wow, she thought. He risked his freedom defending her.

The ringing of her cellphone startled her. It was Tiffany. She let the call go to voicemail. She didn't feel much like talking. Tiffany called right back. Celeste reluctantly answered the call. "Hey girl, what's up?" Celeste answered. Tiffany began to explain that she spoke with Ishmael's brother and that he had court 1st thing Monday morning. "You didn't tell him what I did, did you," Celeste asked? "Girl no. That's none of their business. But they're about to find out," Tiffany fired back.

*Now let's rewind for a little bit. Remember when I said that Celeste was a closet thot? Well, during the week, Celeste is a conservative dressed, naturally hair styled, assistant D.A. for the DeKalb County Prosecutor's Office. Yeah... she was the folks. LOL. But on the weekend, she went through a transformation. It all started when she was attending law school. She needed money so she worked part-time at a clothing store in Decatur on Candler Rd. That's where she met the original thots, Tiffany and ShonDrika. The girls took Celeste under their wings and pulled her out of her Midwestern shell. Now, back to the story. *

1st Appearances and Arraignments were usually pretty routine for Celeste. This morning, however, was far from routine. Celeste arrived at the courtroom early like she always did. She immediately retrieved his case file and poured through it. He was being charged with two counts of Felony Aggravated Assault. With the prior he had on his record he'd do prison time for sure if convicted. Ishmael was wise to hire a lawyer to defend him. Not that it mattered because she wasn't going to let it get that far.

As court began its session there were a few cases ahead of Ishmael's. Celeste noticed Ishmael sitting with his Attorney and discussing his case. He hadn't paid any attention to her or even looked her way, probably because he didn't recognize her. He wore a very nicely tailored black pinstriped suit. Those lips of his did something to her. She turned back around in her chair and pressed her legs together. "Lord help me!" she whispered to herself.

She gave out generous plea deals as she whisked through her caseload. The judge was a little puzzled but paid no real attention. She just wanted to get to Ishmael's case and be done. The clerk called Ismael's case number. He and his lawyer walked toward the podium and listened as the judge read the details of the case. "Mr. Hardwick you're being charged with 2 counts of Aggravated Assault. How does your client plead," the judge asked the attorney? "He pleads not guilty, your honor," he replied.

Just as the judge was about to set a date for trial, Celeste interrupted. "Excuse me your honor, but the state wishes to drop all charges against Mr. Hardwick," she declared. The judge looked puzzled and asked her to explain. Celeste took a deep breath and addressed the court. "Your honor, on the night in question, I just so happen to be a witness to the incident that Mr. Hardwick has been charged in. From what I witnessed Mr. Hardwick was acting in self-defense.... on my behalf."

Celeste glanced over at Ismael and smiled. Ishmael's jaw dropped open and his eyes widened with surprise. The judge chuckled and said to Ishmael, "Mr. Hardwick I see you've met CeCe? Ms. Braithwaite left a case file in my office one Friday afternoon and I had to meet her here later that evening to return it to her. That was my 1st time meeting Ms. CeCe. I must say my brother that I was quite surprised as well." With that the judge grabbed her gavel and yelled out, "case dismissed, you're free to go."

Ishmael was speaking with his attorney when Celeste walked out of the courtroom. "Could you give us a minute," Celeste asked his lawyer? "I never got a chance to properly thank you for stepping in that night. And I hate how things ended up for you because of me," she stated. Ishmael grabbed her by the hand and said, "I want to thank you for stepping up for me in there. Can I please take you to dinner or something to show you, my appreciation? I have to go to

B'more for a couple of days to get my daughter but when I get back, I'm all yours." Celeste began to smile and blush a little. "Yes. I'd like that very much," she answered. Celeste returned to the courtroom and Ishmael exited the building.

Four days later...

Celeste was sitting at her desk going over some upcoming cases and eating her lunch which consisted of a honey bun and a vente mocha frappe' or however you pronounce them shits. She texted Tiffany and they planned their weekend outings. They decided to go to the mountains up in Dahlonega. Tiffany's uncle owned a cabin up there and always told her she could use it whenever she liked. Well just so happens that she got the key from him and neither one of them had anything on her personal schedule. "Girl yes. After the week I've had, I would love to kick back, read a little and drink a lot," Celeste said. Tiffany replied. "Cool. We'll meet at your place around 6 and since you own a Jeep, you can drive." Click! Tiffany hung up without saying goodbye like she usually does when she's being petty.

As the day drew to a close Celeste made some last-minute notes for next week and began to gather her belongings. She was walking out of her office headed to the bathroom when she heard her cell phone buzzing. It was a text from an unknown number the simply read, "Good afternoon, madam prosecutor." Celeste immediately got excited. "Good afternoon Mr. Hardwick. How are you?" – "I'm good. Can you talk? I hate texting. I just didn't know if you were in court or not." – "Sure. But give me about 10 minutes. I need to take care of something." – "Cool. 10 minutes..."

Ishmael waited a few extra minutes before calling her. He sat on his sofa, kicked his feet up, and called her phone. "What took you so long, sir," she jokingly answered. - "I do apologize. I had to see my daughter off. She's going over to Candace's for the weekend to chill out with her cousins. They haven't seen each other in a while." – "Oh ok. How long is she here for? I'd love to meet her." – "I actually just got custody of her. Her mom died in a car wreck a year ago and Tiara has been living with her grandparents until I could get myself settled here in Georgia." – "Oh wow, so you're a single dad?" – "Yes. Is that a problem?" – "Oh no not at all. I think it's commendable that you're stepping up and making things work out for her. If there's any way, I can help out with her just let me know." - Cool. Will do. So, what do you have planned for the night?" – "Funny you should ask," Celeste replied.

"My friends and I are going to the mountains for a couple of days. You should come. It'll be fun," Celeste said. Ishmael thought for second. "Are you sure? I don't want to be out of place," he returned. - "It'll be fine. I'll let the girls know I'm bringing a plus 1. We're meeting at my house around 6:30p this evening. I'll text my address." Ishmael said, "Ok then. I'll see you ladies at 6:30. Talk to you then." – "Ok. Bye." Both of them had big ass smiles on their faces.

By the time Ishmael arrived everyone had already made it and they were standing outside talking. They all said their hellos and loaded up the jeep for the trip. Tiffany, being the friend that she is said, "CeCe why don't you let Ishmael drive since we are going to the mountains and I'm sure that a man like him could handle those curvy roads better than any of us." "You know, she's got point," Ishmael jokingly agreed. Celeste handed him the keys and rolled her eyes at Tiffany.

The crew had a lit time on the way up to the mountains. Ishmael and CeCe sat up front and chatted while Tiffany and ShonDrika sat in the back and moderated the impromptu date. They grilled Ishmael about his life, his likes and dislikes and he grilled them about CeCe. Celeste was embarrassed most of the ride but it was all good fun. Tiffany was being extra petty and created a group text with the ladies and sent potential questions for Ishmael. By the time they arrived at the cabin the final text read, "APPROVED!!"

They all got settled into the cabin and Ishmael insisted on sleeping on the couch. "Well damn," exclaimed Tiffany. "He doesn't have to stay in my room. We barely know each other," said Celeste. "Well, Drika and I will take the rooms on the east side of the cabin and Celeste can have the other room all by her damn self," Tiffany stated. "You are so damn petty," replied Drika. Ishmael pulled his Pelican case into the kitchen and set it up. "I meant to ask you what's in that case," asked Celeste? "Dinner and drinks are on me. 45 minutes," he replied.

The cabin was situated on a hillside overlooking the lake. After dinner Ishmael and Celeste took their drinks down by the lake where there was a beautiful gazebo complete with lounge chairs and fire pit. They sat down and just looked at the water. It was mesmerizing and hypnotic. Lights from distant cabins beamed through the trees. The air was quiet, and the atmosphere was erotically seductive. Celeste placed her hand on his. "How's Tiara doing since moving?" – "She's coming along pretty good. She's a little trooper. I think she was happier about seeing her cousins than actually moving with me." They laughed and sipped. Something about tonight felt magical, thought Celeste.

They talked for hours. Before they knew it, it was almost 2 a.m. They made their way back up to the cabin. Celeste looked Ishmael in the eyes and said, "I never properly thanked you for defending me that night." Ishmael pulled her close and planted a knee-weakening kiss on Celeste. She could feel him growing and it made her wet. Celeste had not been in a relationship since grad school. Well... She felt it was time to end this dry-spell.

They left a trail of clothes from the kitchen to the bedroom. *All Over Again* by Leela James saturated the room. Ishmael was gentle. His soft strong hands glided over body like wind over silk. Celeste was nervous and excited at the same damn time. She lay there trembling from anticipation. Her sweet spot was throbbing and getting juicier as he slowly kissed her body. He paid very close attention to her.

Memorizing every pressure point she had and those she didn't even know she had, he began licking and kissing her thighs. This made her lose it. His locs added to the sensation as they played with her legs. Before she knew it, she climaxed. Ishmael lightly kissed her clit. Slowly he ran his tongue up and down her cocoa lily. She tried to escape the pleasure, but Ishmael gripped her thighs and pulled her back. He buried his tongue deeper into her. She grabbed a handful of her afro and her eyes rolled towards the back of her head. He sucked and slurped on her for what seemed to be forever. She wrapped her legs around his shoulders. The ecstasy was amazing. Her mind was swirling and every nerve in her body responded to his every touch.

Ishmael moved in for part 2. He kissed her soft supple breasts with care and focus. Celeste couldn't take it any longer. *Tank's When We* hit the air. She reached down and took hold of Ishmael's royal staff and pulled him into her. Just the head, that's all he gave her in the beginning. His strokes rode the beat of the music. It was just enough to make her bust all over him. He dove deeper and deeper. Ishmael wanted her to know just how grateful was. He tapped that spot over and over. Celeste was mentally floating in midair. She came more times and harder than she ever had. She rolled him over and lay on his chest. Like the pistons on a locomotive, she put that pussy on him. Celeste kissed his neck and chest. Ishmael gave her a bear hug and held her tight. Like a beautifully choreographed dance they both exploded.

Ishmael was locked in. He hadn't felt like this about a woman since the death of Tiara's mom. Celeste drifted off to sleep. Ishmael stroked her curly fro and kissed her forehead. It's been a long time since he let his guard down and maybe this time it was worth it. Life is full of surprises and unexpected blessings. As for Celeste, it could be nothing or it could be everything. Ishmael was game to see what the future held for both of them.

Chronicle 5

Hot Springs... A Drive thru the Country

The crowd size at Ginnie Springs was fairly moderate. Lifted pickup trucks were lined up as if they were on display at a country boy truck rally. American flags waved through the air as, Try That in A Small Town by Jason Aldean, surfed the calm breeze. Pierce had reluctantly agreed to be the designated driver for this outing with the fellas. His childhood buddies, Corbin, sat up front while Rick and Clay sat in the backseat of the twin cab Silverado. Corbin was meeting his girlfriend and a few of her friends at the springs for a day river tubing and relaxation.

Tami, who was Corbin's girlfriend of 3 years, was accompanied by her good friends and neighbor, Kelly Ann, Miriam, and Becca. Tami had parked her open-air Jeep Wrangler under a huge

Oaktree with lots a shade. She texted her location to Corbin as the ladies gathered their things in preparation for their day on the water. Pierce pulled up next to them and the crew dismounted the vehicle. Corbin and Tami hugged and indulged in a rather raunchy kiss. As Corbin grabbed 2 hands full of ass cheeks everyone shouted, "Get a room. Damn!"

As the introductions were being made, Pierce and Kelly-Ann locked eyes. "Hey, I'm Pierce." "Hi, I'm Kell-Ann." Kelly-Ann couldn't help but notice his familiar military flag tattoo on his right forearm. "Did you serve?" She asked. "Yeah, I was in the Army." He replied. "So is my brother. He's deployed in Africa right now, though," She stated. She also noticed his extremely chiseled physique. She thought to herself, "this mother fucker looks like a Greek god in a tank top, cargo shorts, and a ball cap." Hot damn!

Tami's crew was crazy and seemed to be pretty easy going. The vibe was good as they made their way to the float ramp at Devil Spring. This was Tami's 8th or 9th time at the springs. She'd come with her family on weekend getaways. So, she took the opportunity to give everyone the rundown and particulars about Ginnie Springs. As they arrived at the float release, everyone immediately recognized a Florida celebrity, OMG It's Wicks. He was at the springs filming a segment for his popular show about Florida and all it has to offer. He was friendly and engaging and invited everyone to take a groupie with him. He gave everyone high-fives and fist bumps and sent them on their way with his motto, "And that's on Florida."

The water was crystal clear and warm. The beautiful blues river had a nice calm current, perfect for a lazy day of tubing. The fellas brought a huge cooler full of beer, water, and soda… and a few edibles and some bud for float. The ladies brought chicken wings and other snacks. Rick and Clay cleverly hooked all of their floats together using carabiners and zip ties. Even though Clay was the only black guy in the group, he proudly stated, "now that's some mighty fine redneck ingenuity right there, buddy." Everyone burst into laughter as they drifted down river.

The springs were very calming. The scenery was breathtaking. They came across underwater caverns where scuba divers were exploring their mystic depths. As the gang got acquainted with one another and laughed and cracked jokes, they saw some awesome sites as well. They drifted pass alligators, a school of otters, and even a few manatees.

Corbin took this opportunity to get a little playtime with Tami. As they cuddled together on their raft, Corbin slowly ran his finger across her right nipple and slowly made his way down her stomach. Tami leaned back in their deluxe raft and spread her legs… just slightly enough for Corbin to slide her already wet panties to the side. He gently graced her slippery cunt from her clit to her throbbing little badger hole.

To be continued...

About the Author

C. Baby grew up in West Palm Beach, FL and had an insatiable love for reading as a child. As an adult, he began his career in the music industry where he curated slow jam mix CDs titled The Milky Way.

Over the years C, Baby heard about several sensual experiences from his customers. Thus, leading him to put together the most provocative collection of erotica known as The Milky Way Chronicles.

His goal is to usher in the return of chivalry and femininity… because these crucial social elements seem to be all but lost in today's couple's interactions.